Copyright © 2012 Hallmark Licensing, LLC

Published by Hallmark Gift Books, a division of
Hallmark Cards, Inc., Kansas City, MO 64141

Editor: Emily Osborn
Art Director: Chris Opheim
Designer: Mary Eakin
Production Designer: Dan Horton

Photo Stylist: Betsy Gantt Stewart
Set Builder: Randy Stewart
Photo Retoucher: Greg Ham
Project Coordinator: Jennifer Fisher
Photographer: Jake Johnson
Storyboard & Character Development: Karla Taylor
Character & Prop Designers: Ken Crow, Ruth Donikowski,
Rich Gilson, and Susan Tague

ISBN: 978-1-59530-549-7
SKU: XKT1053

Printed and bound in China
MAY13

A Gift For:

_____

From:

_____

How to Use Your Interactive Story Buddy®

1. Activate your Story Buddy by pressing the "On / Off" button on the ear.
2. Read the story aloud in a quiet place. Speak in a clear voice when you see the highlighted phrases.
3. Listen to your Story Buddy respond with several different phrases throughout the book.

Clarity and speed of reading affect the way Jingle® and Bell® respond. They may not always respond to young children.

Watch for even more Interactive Story Buddy characters. For more information, visit us on the Web at Hallmark.com/StoryBuddy.

I Reply ™
TECHNOLOGY

Hallmark's **I Reply Technology** brings your Story Buddy® to life! When you read the key phrases out loud, your Story Buddy gives a variety of responses, so each time you read feels as magical as the first.

Jingle and Bell's
Christmas Star

By Deborah Welky Miles

Hallmark

Andrew and Jingle looked out the window. It had been snowing for three days and three nights, and the ground was covered in a deep, fluffy blanket of snow.

They couldn't wait to go into town, where Pineville's giant Christmas tree was waiting to be decorated. Jingle felt very happy.

But Jingle's new neighbors, Sofia and Bell, were not happy at all. They had planned to fly to Palm City for Christmas, but their flight was canceled because of all the snow.

Sofia and Bell had just moved to Pineville, and they were still getting used to their new home. They missed their friends. They also missed the sunny weather. It never snowed in Palm City.

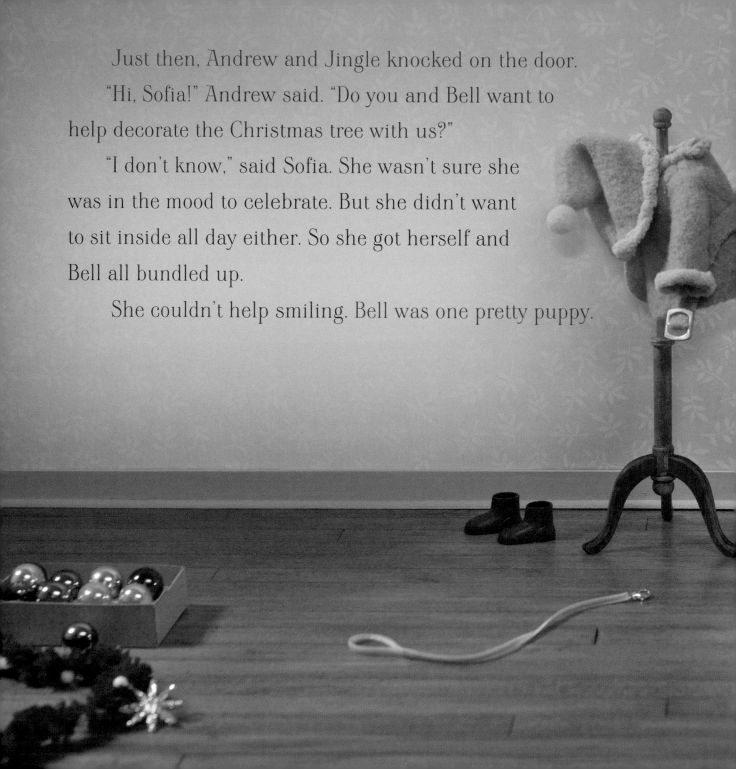

Just then, Andrew and Jingle knocked on the door.

"Hi, Sofia!" Andrew said. "Do you and Bell want to help decorate the Christmas tree with us?"

"I don't know," said Sofia. She wasn't sure she was in the mood to celebrate. But she didn't want to sit inside all day either. So she got herself and Bell all bundled up.

She couldn't help smiling. Bell was one pretty puppy.

Andrew giggled. "I guess you two still aren't used to the snow!"

Jingle was used to the snow, and he loved it! In fact, when he heard the word, he sprinted down the sidewalk. But Andrew called after him, "Jingle, stay!" And Jingle did.

While they walked, Jingle showed Bell where his bird friends lived. He taught her how to chase some squirrels. He even showed her how to help their neighbor shovel her driveway. Mrs. Carlson said, "Jingle, you're such a good dog!"

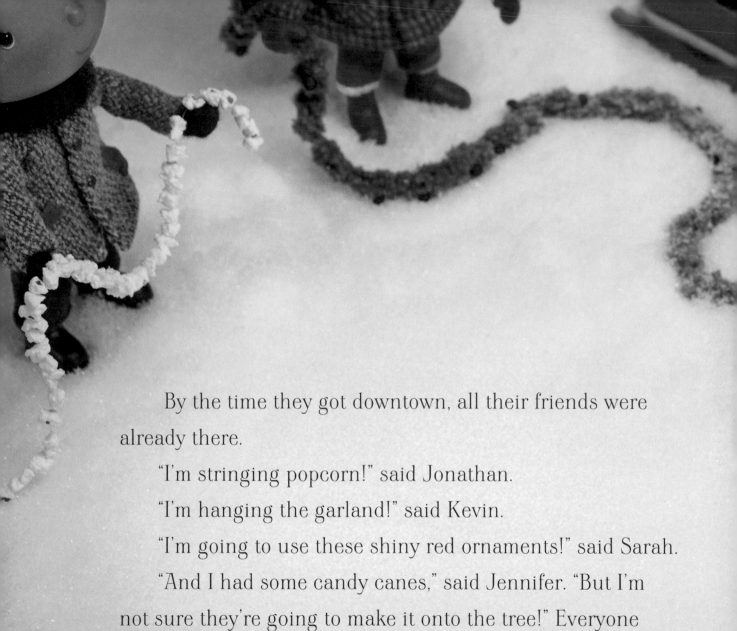

By the time they got downtown, all their friends were already there.

"I'm stringing popcorn!" said Jonathan.

"I'm hanging the garland!" said Kevin.

"I'm going to use these shiny red ornaments!" said Sarah.

"And I had some candy canes," said Jennifer. "But I'm not sure they're going to make it onto the tree!" Everyone laughed, and that made Bell smile.

While everyone worked on the tree, the dogs played with
Jennifer's cat, Mittens. She batted the garland in Bell's mouth
while Jingle tried to catch it.

They were having such a good time, it made Jingle want to sing.

Suddenly, a big red truck turned noisily onto the street.

"What's that for?" asked Sofia.

Andrew smiled. "Every year, someone gets to ride to the top of the Christmas tree and put up the star."

"Wow!" Sofia was excited. She hoped it could be her.

"Who'll be our star-topper this year?" asked the driver
in a jolly voice. "How about you, Andrew?"

Andrew had always wanted to put the star on the
tree. But he said, "My friends, Sofia and Bell, just moved
to Pineville. I think they should do it."

Sofia looked very surprised—and very happy.
That made Bell smile.

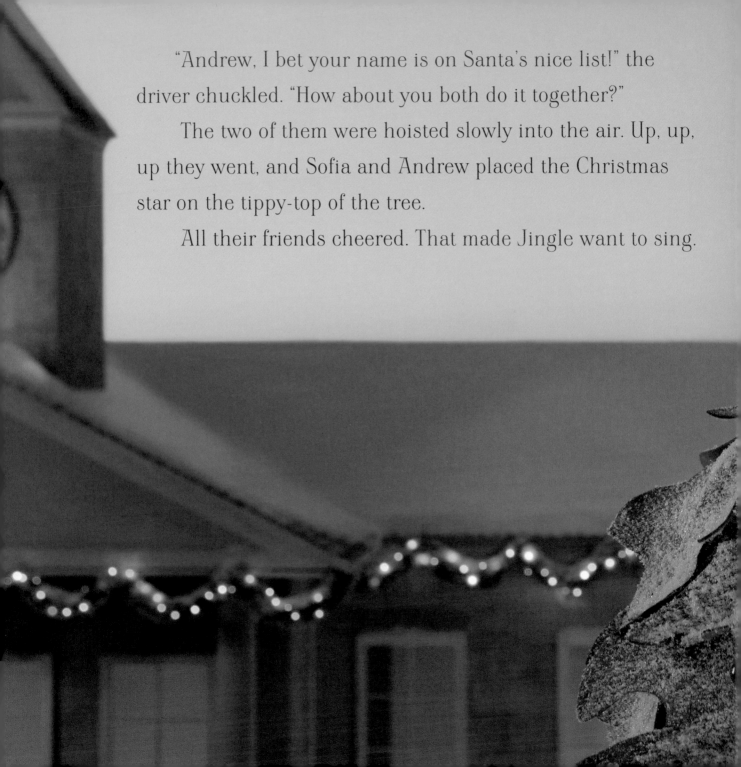

"Andrew, I bet your name is on Santa's nice list!" the driver chuckled. "How about you both do it together?"

The two of them were hoisted slowly into the air. Up, up, up they went, and Sofia and Andrew placed the Christmas star on the tippy-top of the tree.

All their friends cheered. That made Jingle want to sing.

The truck driver gave a quick wink, and—almost magically—all the lights lit up at once.

"That was really nice of you to share your turn, Andrew," Sofia said. "Bell, can you say thank you?"

"Merry Christmas!" said Andrew.

And suddenly, Sofia remembered that there was something very important that she was supposed to do. She waved goodbye to everyone and bent down to pet Jingle's ears. "Jingle, I've got to go home."

When Sofia got back, she wrote a Christmas card to her friends in Palm City. She told them she hoped to see them soon. Bell even signed her name, too.

Sofia bundled up again and headed out to the mailbox. Soon, a light, sparkly snow began to fall.

"You know," said Sofia, "I think I like this kind of Christmas." That made Bell smile.

As they passed their neighbor's house, they saw Andrew and Jingle at the window.

"See you tomorrow!" called Sofia. Bell barked good-bye to her new friends.

And Jingle felt very happy.

Did you have fun with Jingle® and Bell®?
We would love to hear from you!

Please send your comments to:
Hallmark Book Feedback
P.O. Box 419034
Mail Drop 215
Kansas City, MO 64141

Or e-mail us at:

booknotes@hallmark.com